Lloyd Mifflin

The slopes of Helicon and other poems

Lloyd Mifflin

The slopes of Helicon and other poems

ISBN/EAN: 9783743303362

Manufactured in Europe, USA, Canada, Australia, Japa

Cover: Foto ©Andreas Hilbeck / pixelio.de

Manufactured and distributed by brebook publishing software
(www.brebook.com)

Lloyd Mifflin

The slopes of Helicon and other poems

THE SLOPES OF HELICON

AND OTHER POEMS

BY

LLOYD MIFFLIN

AUTHOR OF "AT THE GATES OF SONG"

The best of this kind are but shadows
— SHAKESPEARE

𝕱llustrateð

BOSTON
ESTES AND LAURIAT
MDCCCXCVIII

And trust me while I turned the page
  And tracked you still on classic ground,
  I grew in gladness till I found
My spirits in the golden age.
— TENNYSON

CONTENTS

I. THE SLOPES OF HELICON

PAGE

THE SLOPES OF HELICON 1
ARIADNE IN NAXOS 19
THE DETHRONED 21
FROM MOSCHUS 24
POLYPHEMUS TO ULYSSES 25
WITH WINGÈD STEPS 26
CALLIOPE 27

II. PASTORALS

IN CLOVER BLOOMS 31
THE HILLS 32
TO A FARMER — POOR AND OLD 35
THE CARDINAL-BIRD 36
IN THE FIELDS 37
EPIGÆA 39
IN THE PEACH ORCHARD 40
BIRDS AND THE POET 41

CONTENTS

	PAGE
THE LOCUST-TREES	43
BEFORE DAWN	44
FAREWELL, YE FIELDS	45
MANDRAGORA	47
WINTER'S HERE INDEED	48

III. SONNETS

FROM THE BATTLEMENTS	53
TWILIGHT FROM THE LAWN	54
THE TRIO	55
NOVEMBER	56
SUMMER'S SOUNDS	57
THE PROCESSION	58
A CATTLE PICTURE BY CUYP	59
THE VICTOR	60
OPENING OF THE URNS	61
THE STORM-CLOUDS	62
APRIL THE TWENTY-THIRD	63
LOOKING AT THE WEST	64
THE SEASONS	65
AND THEY SHALL SEE HIS FACE	66
DAWN IN ARQUÀ	67
HOMEWARD BOUND	68

IV. BENEATH THE RAVEN'S WING

IN THE CYPRESS SWAMP	71
A WINTER TWILIGHT	72
YOLANDE	73
CALIBAN	77

CONTENTS

		PAGE
THE BIVOUAC	. . . .	80
THE DEAD QUEEN'S LOVER	. . . . .	81
THE LAND OF NEVERMORE	. . . . .	83
AVENGED	. . . .	85

V. ARROWS OF EROS

OH, NOT ON THE FIELD	. . . . . .	89
THE CAPTIVE	. . . .	90
HER ROSES	. . . .	91
LOVERS IN THE LANE	. . . . . .	92
SIRENS	. . . .	93
THE MOON-SHIP	. . . .	94
BETRAYED	. . . .	95
IN PALL-MALL	. . . .	96
THE LUNCH AL FRESCO	. . . . . .	97
A FRIEND NO MORE	. . . . . .	98
THE LIGHT WITHIN	. . . . . .	99
MY SOURCE OF LIGHT	. . . . . .	100
TAKE BACK YOUR WORDS	. . . . .	101
BY THE FROZEN RIVER	. . . . . .	102
FAR FROM THE DAWN	. . . . . .	103
FROM DAWN TILL DUSK	. . . . .	104
WHERE HAVE THEY GONE	. . . . .	105
IN DREAR NOVEMBER	. . . . . .	106
GO ON WITH THE PLAY	. . . . . .	107
THE CRESCENT	. . . .	108

VI. MINOR CHORDS

BLIGHT	. . . .	111

CONTENTS

ABOVE THE TREES . . . . . .
HOLLYHOCKS . . . .
THE KNIGHT, THE MAID, AND THE MINSTREL
THE SINGER . . . .
LONGFELLOW . . . .
THE WATCHER . . . .
TO A BABY . . . .
A WINTER DIRGE . . . . . .
ROLAND TO THE NUN . . . . .
BEYOND THE HILLS . . . . .
BENEATH THE PALM . . . . .
THE ROAD . . . .
THEY BRING THEIR FLOWERS . . .
MY FATHER AT EIGHTY . . . . .
A POET'S BOOKCASE . . . . .
THE ANNIVERSARY . . . . . .
MY LADY FAIR . . . . . .
O WHAT IS SONG . . . . . .
THE BRIDE OF THE SEA . . . . .
THE WING OF DEATH . . . . .
O EARTH . . . .
ODE TO THE MEMORY OF KEATS . . .
THE IDEALISTS . . . . . .
MARINERS . . . .
ACROSS THE YEARS . . . . . .
FOOTFALLS ON THE STAIRS . . . .

ILLUSTRATIONS

PAGE

PORTRAIT OF THE AUTHOR
From a Photograph, — Feb., 1898 . . . *Frontispiece*

THE SLOPES OF HELICON   From pen drawing by L. M.
Where Cyparissus shot the stag 9

WITH WINGÈD STEPS   From pen drawing by L. M.
Oh, not by Arethusan fountains fair 26

THE HILLS   From pen drawing by T. MORAN, N.A.
But high upon some cloudy crest 34

FAREWELL, YE FIELDS   Drawing by T. MORAN, N.A.
Nor mark the slant sun tip the tasselled corn . . . 45

THE SEASONS   From pen drawing by T. MORAN, N.A.
And worshipped Autumn on her misty crest 65

THE LAND OF NEVERMORE   By T. MORAN, N.A.
And gracious girlhood bloomed and blossomed there . . 83

BETRAYED   From pen drawing by T. MORAN, N.A.
Sink down, O lurid sun 95

BY THE FROZEN RIVER   Drawing by T. MORAN, N.A.
And Winter reigns where Summer failed 102

BEYOND THE HILLS   From drawing by T. MORAN, N.A.
Is there no balm of sweet repose 127

ODE TO THE MEMORY OF KEATS   By T. MORAN, N.A.
And softer than the sound of waters falling 143

THE SLOPES OF HELICON

Among the faint Olympians
        — HYPERION

———•———

The Slopes of Helicon

TO MARZIO DI COLONNA

I

O FRIEND, though now 't is many a day
    Since o'er the blue Ionian sea
    Our sails took wing from Italy,
And in th' Ægean's rocky bay
Were furled, yet bear, though late, from me
    One reminiscent lay;

II

From me, who, under snow-clad trees
    Here on the Pennsylvania hills,
    Across the years of joys and ills
Look back, and seem to hear the breeze
Once more above Idalian rills
    Beyond the Cyclades —

I

»

III

Beyond those sapphire isles asleep,
   Seen in alternate glow and gloom —
   Faint Tenos, bathed in purple bloom;
And Delos, wanderer of the deep;
With Naxos, Ariadne's tomb;
   And Melos, blue and steep.

IV

Remember, how, beneath the pine,
   Upon Hellenic slopes we lay —
   Where beauty consecrates decay,
Mantling the ruin with her vine —
We thought the earth ethereal clay,
   The Olympian air, divine.

V

And on idyllic hills of green,
   Recall how long it kept aloof —
   That spot the wingèd courser's hoof
First struck, — and how, when later seen,
We quaffed, to put it to the proof,
   The Attic Hippocrene.

VI

And after we had drunken there,
    We fancied all the landscape teemed
    With shapes of which we long had
        dreamed,—
Of god and goddess passing fair,
Whose immemorial forms still gleamed
    Across that finer air.

VII

'T was then, below the rustling trees,
    In shadowy copse across the lawn,
    We peered, to mark some Nymph or
        Faun;
And as a balm for missing these —
Still there, but from our sight withdrawn —
    We heard the Hybla bees.

VIII

We felt the aura Zephyr brings;
    Then Cupid in the shade espied
    Asleep, his quiver by his side
Folded beneath his purple wings; —
Heard murmurs in the air that vied
    With Heliconian strings:

3

IX

Not murmurs of the mundane years,
    Nor song of any mortal bird,
    But sounds the old Olympians heard —
And still ecstatic Poet hears —
A rhythmic pæan, void of word,
    A music of the spheres.

X

Then from above the slumberous lea
    We gazed upon the ancient sky;
    Saw him who to the sun would fly,
Far in the blue's immensity
Pause, wingless, and with one last sigh
    Drop in th' Icarian sea.

XI

We marked a god a maid pursue —
    Back from his brow his yellow hair
    Glowed like a sunset cloud in air —
And as he clutched her, swift from view,
The Naiad, like to laurel fair,
    A Hamadryad grew.

XII

Then saw we him who on that isle
 Renounced the blare of war's alarms,
 And, overpowered by her charms —
The goddess of the heart of guile —
Lapped in the lilies of her arms
 Forgot the world awhile.

XIII

Remember, then, behind us stirred,
 From unseen dells beyond the cove,
 Gay Bacchic chantings, interwove
With flutings sweeter than a bird;
When, out before us from the grove,
 A Satyr, sudden, skirred.

XIV

He stopped beside us as he danced, —
 Stopped short, and prick'd a caprine
  ear
Beyond his budding horns, to hear
The clang of cymbals that advanced
Breeze-borne, as from some charmèd sphere,
 To us ward, so it chanced.

5

XV

A roistering rout filed by our side;
    The flushed Bacchantes, ruddy-fair,
    Wove vine-leaves in their tawny hair;
A youth, upon a leopard pied,
'Mid scent of grapes that lingered there,
    Triumphantly did ride.

XVI

Lured to the spot, as they passed by,
    The goat-foot Pan came from the
        meads,
    And seeing Syrinx through tall weeds,
Gave chase all ineffectually;
Then, sullen, wrought that pipe of reeds
    Among the tussocks high.

XVII

While, in the rocky uplands near,
    From undergrowths of laurel cool,
    We heard a voice which did befool
The rapt attention of the ear,
When he of Thespis, in the pool,
    Dropped his pathetic tear.

6

XVIII

And then, upon a sea of blue,
    We watched the curled foam gather
        white,
    Where, to a goddess exquisite,
Slowly the willing waters grew;
While cupids, winged, o'erhead were bright
    With Love's rubescent hue.

XIX

And further, on the Libyan main,
    Chained to a cliff, and like to die,
    We saw a naked beauty lie;
When, through the air above the plain,
He with the Gorgon's head went by,
    And broke her ruthless chain.

XX

Then saw we him of Ocean born,
    Whose crime and passion was to know,
    Alone upon Caucasian snow
Calm and defiant, though forlorn;
Godlike — with genius on his brow —
    Filled with immortal scorn!

7

XXI

We marked a misty peak in air,
  Where clouds of sulphurous smoke
    upcurled;
  While the brute giant seaward hurled
Rock after rock in his despair,
The Ithacan his sails unfurled,
  And left him, eyeless, there.

XXII

Recall that sound as of a lute,
  When from the empyrean deep,
  We saw the eagle downward sweep,
And, as we gazed in wonder mute,
Bear up a lad from 'mid his sheep,
  Who dropped a shepherd's flute;

XXIII

And though full slowly, all around,
  We searched the uplands where it fell,
  O'er many a flowery hillock-swell
That rises on that classic ground,
Yet, on those slopes of asphodel,
  Nor pipe nor flute we found!

8

Where Cyparissus shot the stag

XXIV

And then that cypress, there, alone, —
  The while our steps began to lag
  In toiling to the rocky crag
Whereon it made its throne —
Where Cyparissus shot the stag —
  Began to sigh and moan.

XXV

And still within that mythic air,
  Though somewhat lower in the glade,
  And spreading wide her yewen shade,
Sweet Smilax grew; while beauteous there
Stood Crocus, lover of the maid
  Ephemerally fair.

XXVI

Near by, with large and languorous eyes,
  A wondrous heifer, white and fawn,
  Grazed 'mid the grasses on the lawn;
A Priestess, she, in such disguise,
Whom Jove, within his cloud withdrawn,
  Transformed, to idolize.

9

XXVII

We looked where once Iolchos bloomed;
    And, as the day began to wane,
    Through shadow-rays of sun and rain,
Appeared her temples, all relumed;
While o'er the soft Thessalian plain
    Pelion and Ossa gloomed.

XXVIII

And there we saw the little stream
    Where Jason's sunken sandal lay;
    And, snorting, eager for the fray,
We heard the Centaur stallions scream —
Saw Chiron all his herd display,
    Until the shores did teem:

XXIX

Beheld her, who, beyond the sea,
    With maidens gathering crocus blooms
    In Enna's vale of faint perfùmes,
Walked on demure and dreamily,
Till Dis stole her to queen his glooms —
    The sweet Persephone.

xxx

A daughter of the wave unfurled
    Before us then her wings, bedight
    With all prismatic colors bright ;
Far o'er her head the storm-cloud curled ;
But when she smiled in her delight
    A rainbow spanned the world !

xxxi

And there, like marble, on the slope,
    The primal woman, — white as snows,
    And sweeter than the wildwood rose
Above the banks of heliotrope, —
Who brought to man a thousand woes,
    Yet lures him still with hope.

xxxii

. And turning then, we heard a groan
    From out the gray-green olive borne,
    Piteous and sweet, and so forlorn
'Twould cause to melt a heart of stone ;
Childless, bereft, by sorrow torn,
    She made immortal moan ;

XXXIII

While, like a statue, marble-fair,
    Pallid within the shade she stood, —
    Spouse of Amphion, oh, how could
Latona cause her such despair! —
Still sorrowing for her hapless brood,
    Her wail went down the air.

XXXIV

And near her side, some steps apart,
    Drawn by the bond of poignant woe,
    A Nymph bent o'er her lover low;
And as she saw the cruel dart
That dealt to him that fatal blow,
    She stabbed her breaking heart.

XXXV

Then as the Rose of Ida fell, —
    The crimson on her milk-white throat, —
    We stood grief-struck, till one clear note,
Of soulful song the miracle,
Upon our hearts its pathos smote —
    The voice of Philomel!

XXXVI

To hear her was so rich a boon,
    We, somewhat taken by surprise,
    In pleasèd wonder raised our eyes
To where, from out the copse of June,
Elowed forth th' entrancing ecstasies
    Of that delicious tune!

XXXVII

It died away. . . . We heard a roar,
    And, crashing through snapped under-
        wood,
    With jagged tusks of froth and blood,
Swift past us charged the bristled boar;
The youth lay dead. . . . A wind-flower
        stood
    Upon the forest floor.

XXXVIII

And when had passed the grisly brute,
    And silence settled silverly
    In all the dimples of the lea,
A Muse did then our ears salute, —
A daughter of Mnemosyne, —
    With her melodious lute;

XXXIX

We listened long, but all too soon
    That music ceased that seemed divine :
    Not tinkling bells on distant kine
Are near so sweet, the while the moon
Stoops down beside the sighing brine ͵
    Above the twilight dune !

XL

We saw upon the flowery lea
    A king's fair daughter — beautiful
    More than all lilies which they cull
On blooming banks of Arcady —
Come forth to mount the snow-white bull
    Who bore her o'er the sea.

XLI

And now as day was nearly done,
    And as we scarcely dared to hope
    That light with darkness long could cope,
We paused, and marked Hyperion
Make rosy all the upper slope
    Of dusky Helicon.

XLII

As Daylight faded from the plains,
   Above her own refulgent bier
   We noted that she made appear
Great funeral pyres in her fanes;
And then — and then the Charioteer
   Drove down his crimson lanes!

XLIII

Beyond the dusk horizon far,
   We saw that silver orb arise, —
   Fair as a soul from Paradise,
And lovelier than all others are
That gem the amethystine skies, —
   Bright Hesper — evening star!

XLIV

And they that stood as sentinels
   Upon the ramparts of the air,
   Lit all their lamps, and hung them
       there;
While in gray turret-clouds were bells,
That, as the Twilight sought her lair,
   Tolled out their faint farewells.

XLV

And when the wings of Nox grew wide,
    And she, with all her forehead bowed,
    Rode near us in her sable shroud,
A sleeping youth we dim descried,
And saw the Huntress leave her cloud,
    To lie anear his side.

XLVI

And then a music seemed to wake
    The listening hills and dimmer dales,
    Pathetic as a god's that wails
With rapture while his heart doth ache, —
Her song — th' impassioned nightingale's —
    That floods again the brake!

XLVII

And when was hushed that wondrous tone,
    We heard the sylvan tangle stir,
    And, glimmering in the gloom, saw her —
The purest and the loveliest one,
The last Olympian harbinger —
    Ethereal and alone.

XLVIII

Her spirit made an aureole
    About her wings, which, eagle-wise
    Pulsed, as she panted for the skies;
Her looks were on some heavenly goal;
And from the deeps of star-like eyes,
    Glowed the immortal Soul.

.

XLIX

Then as the Hippocrene divine
    Within us there began to wane,
    Faded each goddess and her fane;
Tottered the temples and the pine;
Vague phantom-figures blurred the plain,
    And fled the hyaline.

L

And now, beside the silver seas,
    Our ship, upon the moonlit bay
    Did slow her dusky anchor weigh ;
The while her sails puffed with the breeze,
We steered her where we thought they lay —
    The dim Hesperides.

LI

Then Brizo, softly on our eyes,
    Laid velvet hands; and in that dream
    Passed and repassed an endless stream
Of godlike, pale Divinities, —
Nor woke we till the Auroran team
    Dazzled the dappled skies.

L'Envoi

LII

Ah, Friend, 't is many a day since then,
    Where, underneath the ilex-trees,
    We saw, or deemed we saw, all these
Beyond the waking eyes of men —
O halcyon days by summer seas,
    That cannot come again!

NORWOOD,
    Dec., 1897.

Ariadne in Naxos

I

So Love is gone! . . . Gone all his passionate sighs,
His rapturous eyes
Intense,
That poured their lava streams
Through dewy meadows of my soul,
Till sense —
As wild grass catches flame —
Leapt into fire, and reason lost control
And dropped her sceptre, vanquished, at his name.

II

So Love is gone! . . . Then how shall I e'er sip
From any lip
That's left,
Less velvet than his own,
My little share of future bliss?
Bereft
Of his most precious breath,
Unsweet will even seem that baby kiss
I count on. Now, life's kindest gift is death.

III

Thou sweet false Theseus — see these empty arms ! . .
By thy white charms
Caressed,
Immeasurable joy we knew,
And felt th' immortal glow,
Close pressed
Like rose-leaves in the rose
That fold into each other as they grow !
Now, walk I here unsandalled, save with woes.

IV

O Nymphs of Naxos, whither did he go ?
Fauns ! if ye know,
Tell me
The way the darling traitor went.
Satyrs ! find me the sod
That he
In passing hath perfumed,
That I may kneel to kiss the path he trod,
And die upon the ground . . abandoned . . doomed !

The Dethroned

THEY were younger than Day or than Night was,
  And younger than Darkness and Doom;
They were born in the prime, after Light was,
  Or ever the world was in bloom.
They were older than Love or than Hate is,
  They were older, by ages, than Death;
Upon Hiddekel, Gihon, Euphrates,
  Ere the nostrils of man knew breath,

And on Pison, where onyx and gold is,
  They looked, ere the Dove and the Flood,
Or the city of Enoch, that old is,
  Rose red as the first brother's blood.
More potential than witches of Endor,
  Oracles, prophets and seers;
And the sheen of their eyes was a splendor
  Unhurt by the havoc of years.

Crowned as queens on gold thrones empyrean,
  With harps and with garments of light,
Still their hymns, throughout æon and æon,
  Came down on the pinions of night, —
Yea, as sweet as to shepherds Chaldean
  When watching in silence their sheep,
From on high fell the peace-giving pæan;
  Or soft as the soothings of sleep ;

Or as harps from shut Paradise portals
  To Dives in sulphurous seas —
Oh, the voice of the shining immortals
  Was sweeter, far sweeter than these !
For the host of them sang — sang together
  At dawn, in the morning of years;
Drunk with bliss, reeled the world in its tether,
  And thrilled to their centres the spheres.

But empty their thrones in the zenith,
    But shattered their sceptres of old —
Now men hear not their voice, and it seemeth
    Men's gods are their ingots of gold —
They were daughters of Darkness and Chaos,
    Were stronger than Famine and Wars;
They had power to save or to slay us;
    Their names were the names of the stars.

From Moschus

PARAPHRASE

When all unruffled sleeps the silent sea,
Outward I look, and love the land no more;
Fain would my feet forever leave the shore
To drift upon that calm serenity.
But when wild ocean thunders angrily,
And torn waves break into white foam, and roar,
Then I, ill pleased, seeking the forest floor,
Love the wind's harping through each swaying
tree.
Ah, he whose life is passed upon the wave,
Whose wandering bark is but a house of death,
Toils through wild dangers to a watery grave:
Me, rather, let the forest lull to dreams,
Low lying on some bank, the boughs beneath,
In calm repose beside the woodland streams.

Polyphemus to Ulysses

TO E. R. T.

REVENGE! Revenge! Ye have shut out the light —
 Burned out my single eye the while I slept;
 But for each tear of blood that I have wept,
 Ye shall give forth a groan. . . . I will incite
The avenging Sea against you, and will smite
 You utterly. . . . Ai! Ai! Not Jove shall intercept
 My gathering wrath, ye treacherous wolves, that
    crept
 In secret to my cave, and made day — night!
Now by my sire Neptune's oozy locks
 And forkèd trident; by the boisterous shell —
 The demi-dolphin Triton's roaring horn —
I swear 't were better ye had ne'er been born;
 For I will whelm you with down-thundering rocks
 Deeper than Trojan plummet ever fell!

With Wingèd Steps

OH, not by Arethusan fountains fair,
　Nor silver rivers running softly fleet;
　Ah, not on mountains trod by fabled feet,
　Though flushed the snowy tops in sunset air ;
I journey not by them — not there — not there !
　On classic ground for me — though that were
　　sweet —
　No need to roam in body, — me who greet
　The deathless white immortals, every-where:

Lovely the vales about me, and the dells,
　And yet I pace not them, as on I tread, —
　For Fancy ever is a conjurer ;
Each footstep falls in azure paths o'erhead,
　And I, entranced, listening to faint-heard bells,
　Wander afar in fields that never were.

Oh, not by Arethusan fountains fair

Calliope

WHAT shall atone for studious days
  Spent at the Muse's cruel side?
  What recompense wilt thou provide
For labor sore in making lays —
One of thy wreathèd bays,
    Calliope?

Think of the long nights spent with thee,
  When other men were glad with wine,
  With woman's love they deemed divine,
While I was lone as islands be
Within a sailless sea,
    Calliope!

Would any wreath thou couldst bestow —
  Albeit all wreaths of thine are vain —
  Repay for half this life-long pain?
Thy laurels for some happier brow;
I heed not laurels now,
    Calliope!

Still wear to me thine ancient frown;
   Be heartless, as thou wast of old,
   And yield me neither rest nor gold;
I scorn thy proffer of renown,
For Death, too, brings a crown,
    Calliope!

PASTORALS

A' babbled of green fields
                    — SHAKESPEARE

In Clover Blooms

I

ROUGH is the road
That Fame would goad
Us ever rudely over; —
How free from care
Yon maiden fair
A-wading through the clover!

II

O restless man,
Thy little span
Why fume and fret it over?
Come here and stroll,
And ease thy soul
While walking through the clover.

III

That golden street
Where hallowed feet
Tread, ever softly, over,
Is far away;
But here, to-day,
Enough for me, the clover!

The Hills

I will lift up mine eyes unto the hills

TO THE MEMORY OF
THE REV. CHARLES WEST THOMSON

I

THOUGH all the fields about my feet
Are beauteous with the frozen sleet,
    And snow the valley fills ;
Not here my spirit stoops and clings,
But there she soars and spreads her wings —
    Above the hills —
    Above the hills !

II

As in her splendor and her sheen
The Spring comes back with all her green,
    To wade through daffodils ;
Turning away, afar I gaze
Across the faint cerulean haze,
    Upon the hills —
    Upon the hills !

32

III

Though in the laurel underbrush
I hear the warble of the thrush
  And all its tender trills ;
Yet oh, the spiritual bells
Within those amethystine dells
  Among the hills —
  Among the hills !

IV

The Summer spreads upon the plain
A thousand sheaves of golden grain
  Anear her waiting mills ;
I turn unto yon barren crags,
They call — they wave their purple flags —
  The phantom hills —
  The phantom hills !

V

When sumptuous Autumn strews the sod
With scarlet vine and golden-rod,
  And every murmur stills ;
E'en then I gaze till vision dims,
Upon those amaranthine rims —
  The dreamy hills —
  The dreamy hills !

33

VI

And when November, dull and sere,
Her lurid sunset spreads, and drear,
    And all the landscape chills;
I turn from this and gladly part;
They lay their hands upon my heart —
    The evening hills —
    The evening hills!

VII

And even after I am old,
In summer, or in winter's cold —
    Come health, or age's ills;
Still let me raise my weary eyes
And rest them on my Paradise —
    The fading hills —
    The fading hills!

VIII

And when they make a grave for me,
Not in the valley may it be
    Beside the meadow rills;
But high upon some cloudy crest,
Closer to heaven I would rest,
    Upon the hills —
    Upon the hills!

But high upon some cloudy crest

To a Farmer — Poor and Old

His form is bended with old age and toil,
  A life-long labor spent upon the sod
That yields him scarcely half enough to eat.

Bear up, brave heart! there is celestial soil,
And by still waters will He lead your feet, —
  There *must* be justice in the halls of God!

The Cardinal-Bird

TO MARY ANDERSON — MADAME DE NAVARRO

THE Cardinal has come again;
  He all the brake salutes;
His music floods the silent glen, —
  Oh, hear him, how he flutes!

From tree to tree his scarlet glows;
  Such beauty rare he brings,
That all the richness of the rose
  Seems lavished on his wings!

In the Fields

JUNE TWENTY-FIRST

WHEN daily greener grows the oats;
When near his nest the red-wing floats,
  And sweetbrier blossoms in the lane;
When freshening wind the wheat-field
    shakes,
And in its billowy rolling makes
  An ocean of the grain:

When rye begins to bend its head,
Fearing the coming reaper dread
  That ruthless o'er it soon shall pass;
When meadow-larks, that on their breast
Carry the dandelion's crest,
  Pipe, in the waving grass:

When from the dimples of the mere
Come distant voices, faintly clear,
  Across the dells of lazuli;
When airs that stir the poplar spray
Bring odors from the heaps of hay
  That on the uplands dry:

37

When wading cows, in cool mid-stream,
Stand by the hour in some dull dream
   Of meadows deep with clover-blooms;
When all the knolls are gold of hue,
When all the silences of blue
   Are heavy with perfùmes:

When, as the shades of evening fall,
We catch the faint reëchoing call
   From moving hayloads on the hill;
When gnats in swarms a-dancing go
Within the golden afterglow
   Where whirls the whippoorwill:

When all the elder-blossoms white,
That skirt the runnel, burst in sight,
   Ah, then we know the time o' year, —
And then, entranced, we raise our eyes
In gladness to the glowing skies, —
   At last the Summer 's here!

Epigæa

INSCRIBED TO

THE MEMORY OF BAYARD TAYLOR

APRIL is coming, and I surely hear,
  On all the mossy slopes and woodland dells,
That elfin music, delicately clear,
  From coral clusters of Arbutus bells.

Sweet, native flower, that lov'st the lowly ground,
  Close to my secret soul in truth thou art ;
The earth-star thou — and yet I have not found
  In all the heavens one dearer to my heart.

Precious thou wast in days that young love gave,
  When sight of thee could make my bosom thrill ;
Oh, might some friend but plant thee on my grave,
  To tell the woods, thy lover loves thee still !

In the Peach Orchard

THE workman in the orchard rows
Picked crimsoned fruit as high as he could reach;
The farmer said, " My favorites are those, —
They're very hard to beat, —
      The ' Mountain Rose.' " ...

The little daughter of the workman passed;
We saw the dew upon her nut-brown feet;
He said, while smiling on us each
With pride a father only knows,
" That is *my* favorite peach —
      My Mountain Rose!"

Birds and the Poet

THE robin that runs through the orchard old,
   Robbing the grass of its tangles of gray;
The lark, with her breast of daffodil gold,
   That drops, like a star, on the meadows of May;
The bluebird that floats from the top of the tree,
   With the flash of the sky on his beautiful wings;
The sparrow that drowns the drone of the bee,
   Where the maple-buds burst, as he madly sings;

The turtle that coos from the bellefleur bare,
   Seeking a nook where the branches will bloom;
And the wren that wakens the somnolent air
   As he mounts with a twig to his resonant room;
These sang to the poet — sang early and late:
   "Wake, indolent wooer, the Spring is for love!
Each songster is making a nest for her mate,
   But where is, O Singer, thy nest, or thy dove?"

Then the poet looked up through the halls of the air,
  To follow the wave of a mystic hand;
And Love went by at his feet in despair,
    While he worshipped that Vision, so white and
      grand.
The dove cooed content as the days rolled around;
    The breeze through the blossoms swept soft as a
      sigh;
The lark thrilled with joy near her nest on the ground,
    But the soul of the poet still sobbed for the sky.

The Locust-Trees

A SUMMER SONG

AH, why will men a-wandering go
   Across the silver seas,
To seek th' Illyrian ilex,
   Or th' pine of Pyrenees;
When here, beneath the shadows,
   They may rest and take their ease,
While the air is filled with perfume
   Of the lovely Locust-trees?

Oh, tell me not of golden boughs
   In far Hesperides, —
There's nothing in the world so sweet
   As drowsing here by these, —
As dreaming 'neath the branches
   When the blooms are full of bees,
In the languorous lotus-odor
   Of the lovely Locust-trees!

Before Dawn

WHY dost thou sing so madly now, O Bird,
  Now, ere the sunrise brings the light? . . .
Ah, these are shreds of music thou hast heard
  In dreams throughout the night!

Nor mark the slant sun tip the tasselled corn

Farewell, Ye Fields

TO THE MEMORY OF H. W. G.

ALAS ! to drink no more the crystal spring
 Where oft I drank beneath the meadow rock
Nor see the blackbird, with his scarlet wing,
 Poise to entice me, on the bending dock;

Nor see the elder, blossoming still in June,
 Whiten the brook-side with its drift of snow;
Nor scan the hill-top till the crescent moon
 Hangs her gold sickle on the orchard bough;

Nor mark the slant sun tip the tasselled corn
 When dawn's flushed cheek grows paler in the sky;
Nor watch the wind — a breath of summer morn —
 Roll the green billows o'er the seas of rye;

Nor wade through odorous swaths the mowers throw,
 Nor hear the music as they whet the scythe;
Nor sight the cradlers, coming all arow,
 The ripe grain sweeping with their swayings lithe;

45

Ah, not again beneath the wildwood boughs,
    To pluck the mountain laurel's roseate stars;
Nor o'er the clover call the lowing cows,
    And watch their coming at the upland bars;

Nor see the oxen, loosened from their load,
    Tread through the twilight o'er the dark'ning wold;
Nor, in the evening, down the dusty road,
    Know the flock coming by the cloud of gold;

Oh! ne'er again to rest beside the sheaves,
    To hail the binders, when their toil is done;
Nor on the grain load, brushed by apple leaves,
    Ride down the long lane at the set of sun:

These peaceful vales no more shall know my feet;
    Some later poet here shall tune his lay;
And still the winds will wave the fields of wheat,
    And still will float the odor from the hay!

Mandragora

THERE 's golden haze in the mellow air,
There 's purple and crimson everywhere,
    East and west;
Gathers the Autumn into her fold,
The wandering leaves of her flocks of gold, —
  So rock me, Earth, oh, rock me to rest!

Struggles the vine through half o' the year,
To ripen each purple, bloomy sphere,
    East and west;
But it ceases now, for its toil is done,
And it waits the warmth of the vernal sun, —
  So rock me, Earth, oh, rock me to rest!

The idle birds in the dreamy haze,
Dream and dream through the amber days,
    East and west;
Must Man, the monarch, forever toil,
Nor learn of the vine, the bird, and the soil?
  Then rock me, Earth, oh, rock me to rest!

Winter's Here Indeed

THE summer's skiffs that lined the shore
Are laid upon the snowy banks
    With many a useless oar.
Where silver minnows played their pranks
By arrow-headed weeds in ranks
Along the marge, they play no more, —
    For Winter's here indeed!

The shifting shadow from the bough
No longer delicately weaves
    Upon the wading cow
The dappled semblance of the leaves;
The ferry-flat, uppiled with sheaves
From island harvests, comes not now, —
    For Winter's here indeed!

And, oh, the plumy islands dim,
So purple and so azure fair,
    That almost seemed to swim
Within the amethystine air —
Like spirits free from every care —
From river's tranquil rim to rim,
    Ere Winter came indeed!

And have they, then, their mooring lost?
Slipped anchor here, and sailed away
  To some more sunny coast?
To some far-off Floridian bay,
Where balmy airs around them play?
Or buried are they by the frost,
  Since Winter's here indeed?

The wild ducks floating by in flocks;
The flying geese with phantom scream;
  The heron on the rocks;
The halcyon, darting down the stream, —
All, all, are vanished as a dream, —
For ice the darling river blocks,
  Since Winter's here indeed.

O April with thy violet eyes,
Come walking down the willowy shores,
  And take us by surprise!
And burst to leaf the sycamores,
And calm the river where it roars,
And herd thy white flocks in the skies, —
  For Winter's here indeed!

SONNETS

Within the sonnet's narrow plot of ground
— WORDSWORTH

From the Battlements

A THOUSAND years, I think, I have been dead,
  And yet I have not seen her.   Can it be
  I am to miss her through eternity, —
  I who on earth thrilled at her lightest tread ?
Among the millions here that ever thread
  These streets of gold, I surely soon shall see
  That soul that died in her virginity, —
  Shall find at last my love long vanishèd.
I feel that I shall know her through disguise
  Of spiritual splendors.   I will stand
  Upon the bulwarks, and will watch and wait.
It *must* be, that within this pearly gate
  Long hath she entered from the dreamless
      land. . . .
  Ah ! I shall know her by her love-lit eyes.

Twilight from the Lawn

TO SAMUEL WADDINGTON, ESQ.

Low in the west the golden crescent's rim
  Sinks slowly in the orange afterglow;
  Pale puffs of steam rise into rings, and go
  Circling in air.   Upon the river's brim
A gleam of silver lingers.   On the limb
  Hoots the lone owl; and, high above, the crow
  Wings to the wood, most wearily and slow;
  The hills are purpling, — dimmer and more dim;
Against the glory of the going light
  Stand the cathedral spires of the pines;
  The swallows, swirling in concentric lines,
Swoop down the ivied chimney for the night;
  While through the pane — a star that doth not
      roam —
  Twinkles the lamp — the Hesperus of home.

The Trio

WITH wings upraised, and trumpet pointed high,
 She poised upon the summit of a cloud;
 " My name is Glory," blew her trump aloud,
 " Who follow in my steps shall never die ! "
Then, at that blare, one rose and fixed his eye
 Upon her, drawing from his skull the shroud,
 And spake with voice, that, tho' it whispered,
  cowed, —
 " Nay, all are mine, forever ! — Death, am I ! "
Thereat a baleful Power filled the air, —
 Shook all the shores of their dominion,
 And cried from out the blackness to them there :
" I am the Vortex named Oblivion, —
 Agèd I was, ere Chaos had begun;
 Glory and Death ! behold *me*. . . . and despair ! "

November

FOR Autumn's splendors now I search in vain;
    The crimson thyrsus of the sumac bud,
    And the haw's berries, dashed with Summer's blood,
    Are dripping in the dull November rain.
No tasselled wigwams of the corn remain.
    All yellow are the streams with swollen flood;
    And on the hill-side road, the golden mud
    Falls from the felloes of the laboring wain.
Above the town, upon its wooded perch,
    With unmarked mounds, the little graveyard lies —
    Watched over by the dove-like Quaker church —
Where sombre pines are pointing to the skies;
    The only mourner now — the pendent birch —
    Drops tears, to-day, above long-buried eyes.

Summer's Sounds

TO H. M., M. D.

ONE listening, in the clover fields can hear
  The mower whet his scythe; and far away,
  O'er lowlands odorous with the new-mown hay,
  The rattle of the reaper sharp and clear.
Across the reedy stretches of the mere
  The grazing horses send their greeting neigh;
  While, 'mid the silences throughout the day,
  The locust's sharp staccato stabs the ear.
Dim shimmering in the heat the violet hills
  Call to us vaguely from a realm of dreams;
  And from the meadow's smooth meandering
     streams,
Come muffled murmurs of the distant mills;
  From upland wheat-fields, as his barns he fills,
  We hear the farmer, calling to his teams.

The Procession

FROM caverns of the countless ages vast,
    Along the twilight of the monstrous sky,
    Huge, gloomy figures, dark with majesty,
    Hooded, mysterious, stalked from out the past.
Slowly they filed, and as I looked, aghast,
    Their distant voices seemed one hollow sigh
    Filled with Remembrance and with Prophecy.
    They peered upon me as a thing outcast,
Frowning reproof athwart th' upbraiding skies;
    No word they spake, but in each cloudy scowl
    The cold aversion of averted eyes
Burned me as fire, and did my soul arraign;
    While from the smouldering orbs beneath each
        cowl,
    I felt the deathless daggers of disdain.

A Cattle Picture by Cuyp

WITH MAN PIPING

LIST! . . . 'tis the cowherd's mellow tones that fill
   The glowing spaces of the golden air,
   While the rich group of kine, with sun-smit hair,
   Dream their dull dream of wadings by the mill.
Tread softly through the grasses, and be still . . .
   Speak not above a whisper — have a care,
   Lest he should cease his flutings ! . . . Notice where
   The shepherds, listening, pause upon the hill;
The very children gaze, and stop their play,
   Bound to the place by music's magic bands. . . .
   O piper of the picture, keep thy hands
Forever on thy flute, as here to-day;
   The world is full of noise, — pipe on, we pray !
   Thy note the spirit hears, and understands.

The Victor

DOWN in the cloudy towers of my sleep
  A dungeon loomed, wherein I heard the tones
  Of those long ages prisoned, — groans on groans;
  And, peering further in the noisome deep,
Wherein no rays of daylight éver créep,
  I saw a skeleton of whitened bones —
  A mighty king and conqueror of thrones —
  Chained to the walls within this donjon-keep:
His crown still blazed upon him, golden-dull,
  Whence, through the dark, glared jewels, tiger-
    eyed.
  In awe I stood, and, trembling, held my breath;
And then a Voice — not his who there had died —
  Hissed from the horror of that hollow skull, —
  "I am the King of kings, undying Death!"

Opening of the Urns

ALONG the reaches of the sunset sea,
  A troop of wingèd Spirits, mystic, fair,
  Dim as the clouds, and dreamy as the air,
  Fluttered from out the twilight down to me :
" The golden vases which we brought to thee,
  Time after time — before thy brow with care
  Was seamed, and, too, since thou hast known de-
      spair —
  Hast thou worked out, with them, thy destiny ?
In the past days that long have vanishèd,
  What hast thou filled them with ? " they softly said.
  And I replied — not without shame and fears —
" Ah, Fate has filled them for me, thro' the years ;
  Lo ! Open them, and see ! " — and bowed my
      head. . . .
  " Alas ! " they sighed, " these urns are full of
      tears ! "

The Storm-Clouds

TO THE

MEMORY OF SAMUEL S. HALDEMAN, LL. D.
Late Professor of Comparative Philology,
University of Penna.

I STAND beside the River as the night
  Unrolls her sombre curtain o'er the day;
  The pyres within the west have paled away
  And only left their embers, dimly bright,
To 'lume the purple hill-top's sullen height;
  Then, from behind the crags, the clouds of
      gray —
  A troop of lions held too long at bay —
  Arise from out their antres in their might,
And low along the mountain ridges prowl,
  Tossing their shaggy manes with lordly roar;
  While, by the lash of lightnings still uncowed,
They, raging and rebellious, long and loud,
  Send many an angry and deep-throated growl
  Rumbling along the caverns of the shore!

April the Twenty-third

(1564–1616)

I AM not proud because I make to bloom
    Each year the hawthorn by the cottage gate;
    Nor that I raise the rose's heart elate
    With thoughts of climbing to my lady's room;
But that, one golden morn, I did illume
    The world with him, — a light to dominate
    And daze all time. It was my envied fate
    To lay him in his cradle and his tomb.
When Nature gave him she became lovelorn,
    Nor would she let him longer here abide;
    And if in memory of the time, men mourn,
Grieving, — "This is the day that Shakespeare
    died,"
    I, April, answer from the Avon's side,
    "This is the day my dearest child was *born!*"

Looking at the West

YE Evening Clouds, on which I sadly gaze,
  Mine eyelids wet with untumultuous tears,
  Because your beauty's poignant pathos sears
  Itself into the soul, the while the ways
Are rich with ruby and with chrysoprase —
  Ye clouds of evening, in those promised years,
  In the great oriel of some grander spheres,
  Shall not your splendor glad our heavenly days?
God's smile it is that floods the sunset sky —
  He cheers us with this parting, lest we might
  Be frighted by the Dark's immensity.
How could we bear the absence of the light,
  Unless, each eve, down-bending from on high,
  He from those Doors of Heaven beamed, "Goo
    night?"

And worshipped Autumn on her misty crest

The Seasons

In youth, I thought that April, azure-dressed,
  Was queen of all the year, her blue eyes beaming
  With earliest love — with passionate glances gleam-
      ing;
  Later, I found in all my errant quest
Nothing so sweet as June; next loved I best
  The rich late Summer, with her harvests teeming,
  Throned on her slopes of gold; then fell I dream-
      ing,
  And worshipped Autumn on her misty crest;
But now the sweetest days seem dull December's,
  For in the darkness of my twilight room,
  I peer into the hearth-fire and the embers,
And see fair visions rising through the gloom, —
  Ah, dearer than all else the heart remembers! —
  Faces of those beloved when in their bloom.

And They Shall See His Face

'T is said that after life, within the sky,
  If we through mercy then are granted grace,
  We there may see the Godhead face to face;
  And this is promised as felicity. . . .
Ye flaming Seraphs round the throne on high,
  Bend down your ever-burning wings apace
  And shade me from that look! Fill all the space,
  Angels, between me and the Deity!
How could I the full blaze of splendor bear
  Unless excess of glory made invisible
  The Godhead? No,—ah, no! Hide me in
    shade! . . .
Not thine, O God, but faces loved full well
  On earth, let *them* look on me ever there,
  Gentle and kind,—and let them never fade.

Dawn in Arquà

INSCRIBED TO HIS MEMORY

(Obiit July 18, 1374)

SICK of mere Fame, and of Rome's Laureate leaf
  His Latin Epic brought him, up he went
  To steep Arqueto, where he found content
  Among th' Euganean Hills — alas, too brief!
His was an irremediable grief.
  That heart so loved, that head so opulent
  Of gold, were long since dust. . . . Silent he bent
  Above those Sonnets in that Golden Sheaf:
Far into midnight, lone he sat, and read
  The *Rime* once again. . . . Oh, bitterest tears
  By age, for love all unrequited, shed! . . .
Then, on that volume slowly sank his head;
  And in the mountain cottage — bowed with years —
  At early morn they found him, cold and dead.

Homeward Bound

As some stray carrier-pigeon onward hies
  O'er alien spire, and dim cathedral dome,
  With weakening pinions, that reluctant roam
  Athwart the high, inhospitable skies;
Famished and faint, with eager, yearning eyes,
  Whirled by the winds above the wild sea's foam,
  Till, at the last, outworn, he gains his home,
  Falls at his mistress's feet, content, and dies:

So unto thee, sweet Mother of all Song,
  Weak and full weary with world-wanderings,
  We wing the trackless deserts of our sky —
Truant to thee, O Poësy, too long —
  We reach thy feet at last with bleeding wings,
  · And fain would nestle near thy heart to die !

BENEATH

THE RAVEN'S WING

They are black vesper's pageants
— SHAKESPEARE

In the Cypress Swamp

I

On his pools that are black
  Is the green
That breeds the ague ache;
As a crown, on his head
  Unclean —
As a crown, on his skull
  Obscene,
Is coiled the copper snake.

II

In the darks of the depths
  Of his damps,
From immemorial time,
In the flare of his dim
  Marsh lamps,
Sits the King of the Realm
  Of Swamps —
Dead, on his Throne of Slime!

A Winter Twilight

A BLEAK, keen twilight, cold and still;
   White fields of gloom below ;
The clover path around the hill
   Hearsed in its pall of snow ;
To brier tangles, scant and bare,
   The shivering snow-birds go ;
A crescent's thin face, full of care,
   Aches in her silver bow ;
The lingering light, in gray despair,
   Sinks melancholy low ;
Afar, two homeless foot-tracks wind
   Into a night of woe,
Where, like a vague dread in the mind,
   Drifts the belated crow.

Yolande

TO SIG. ILARIO SILVIO

I

THE blithe knights name me " Mad Sir Rue,"
For, of the Table Round,
    These eyes of woe
    That dazed the foe,
Bend lowest on the ground.

II

This eagle spirit mounts no more —
    This armor is a-rust —
    Not as of yore
    This soul shall soar —
Her wings are in the dust.

III

And am I crazed, since she, my bride,
    My Yolande, left me here?
    In beauty's pride
    She paled and died,
And glorified a bier!

IV

I hear the sobs that rise for aye
    Above her jewelled pall.
        By night — by day —
        I hear the clay
    Wail on her coffin wall.

V

This fiend that gnaws me — fiend thou art,
    More fell than ghoul or gnome —
        He tears a part
        From out my heart
    And lays it in her tomb.

VI

And when I kneel, as is most meet,
    And cross myself in prayer,
        I hear it beat . . .
        And beat . . . and beat . . .
    Beneath her yellow hair.

VII

At night, when to her grave I pass,
　　Wet with the wailing rain,
　　　　Down in the grass,
　　　　These lips, alas!
　　Call to her — all in vain.

VIII

Yet Yolande knew my voice of old;
　　But now, how can she hear,
　　　　Through fold on fold
　　　　Of glimmering gold
　　That rests about her ear?

IX

I feel that long gold grow and grow.
　　Ah me, what hair she had!
　　　　Dust! . . . Dust! . . . I know —
　　　　Yet were that so,
　　How could I then be glad?

X

Glad am I, when, at evening red,
A music sweet and clear,
Up from the dead,
Floats overhead
And lingers faintly near, —

XI

A voice as soft as angels' are —
A music sweet and strong,
As if afar
A falling star
Had perished into song.

XII

Hear ye no voices soft and low?
Then ye, too, deem me mad, —
I only know . . .
Long . . . long . . . ago
That Yolande made me glad!

Caliban

I

CALIBAN sprawls on the slippery beach
    Beside the slimy sea;
Freckled, misshapen, a dog in speech,
He clutches the mussels in his reach,
    Craunching them greedily.
Of Sycorax, hag, he is the son;
He was littered here as the toads that run
    In caves by the sluttish sea;
What could his dam do but pollute
This unkempt whelp — this monster brute —
    Weed of the impish sea?

II

He sprawls on his belly on the sands
    Along the swashing sea;
The ape, with his long and hairy hands,
    More human is than he:
He swallows the crawling things a-raw,
    The crab, and the dead sea-mew;
He eats the jelly-fish all a-fresh —
    That mass of clotted glue;

He hankers ever for human flesh;
He gloats as he sights the shipwrecked crew,
    For a cannibal is he;
And ever ravenous is his maw
    Beside the carrion sea.

III

His copper skin is blotched and bright,
    And of a sickly hue;
Both of his tusks are yellow-white,
    And one is broke in two;
Twin rows of teeth run round his jaw;
His bite is death, for his gums are blue;
The film on his eye as he leers at you
    Is livid as a snake's.
From the frog's green pool he laps the scum
    Within the marshy brakes —
    No other spring has he;
And as he writhes with ague numb,
He in his torture howls and quakes
    Beside the Python sea.

IV

In the pitch-dark sky the lightnings flash
    Above the roaring sea;
The thunders growl, and the black waves dash
Over the rocks with a roar and a crash,
While he cowers low on the lurid sand
    Flat by the sulphurous sea.
But more than the waves he fears the wand
    Of Prospero, the King; —
    Sea-calf and a slave,
He licks the foot of the meanest thing,
    This slime of the wave,
    This beast of a man, —
        Caliban,
    Scum of the filthy sea!

.

The Bivouac

THE snows are swirled across the skies;
　　Strong blows the blizzard's breath;
The baffled crow all vainly tries
To stem the blast, nor with it vies,
　　But drifts to death.

Then come the terrors of the sleet,
　　Of storm, and wind, and dark;
The blinding snow shall round them beat,
Shall wrap about their freezing feet,
　　And leave them stark!

The Dead Queen's Lover

THE night was dismal and dark
As the moon crept out from a cloud,
Where the king lay awake in his snow-white bed
 As Life might lie in a shroud.

He placed his hand on his heart,
To hear what its beating said,
And it throbbed aloud, through the ominous gloom,
 " Dead ! . . . Dead ! . . . Dead ! "

" O heart ! " he cried, in his pain,
" Why moan like a mateless dove ? "
Yet never a word the heart replied but,
 " Love ! . . . Love ! . . . Love ! "

" Kind Heaven ! " he prayed in his grief,
" Hast thou no balm for woe ? "
And a gnome from the nadir moaned reply,
 " No ! . . . No ! . . . No ! "

" O Soul of my sainted Love,
Shall we meet on the shining shore ? "
But a sigh sobbed down through the sky above,
    " No more ! . . . No more ! . . . No more ! "

" Cold dagger, then, thou art my Bride, —
Come lighten the burthen of breath ! "
And the jaws of Darkness dripped with blood,
    As he leapt to the throne of Death.

And ghastly and pale is the night,
As the moon shudders under a cloud ;
For is it a king on his snow-white couch,
    Or a corpse, in a crimsoned shroud ?

And gracious girlhood bloomed and blossomed there

The Land of Nevermore

THERE was a land beyond all others sweet,
  Upon whose golden shore
We trod triumphant with our buoyant feet;
Beauteous the balmy days, yet oh, how fleet, —
  The Land of Nevermore!

The royalties of boyhood, frank and fair,
  Spread round their wealth galore;
And gracious girlhood bloomed and blossomed
    there;
Within that land no sorrow came, nor care, —
  The Land of Nevermore!

One day Love wandered down the leafy lane
  Where he ne'er came before;
And guileless honor walked without a stain,
For in that land there was no love profane, —
  The Land of Nevermore!

Oh, for the faith that flamed up like a pyre, —
   The strength of soul each bore!
Ah, for the glow, the passion, and the fire!
For that was all a land of high desire, —
   The Land of Nevermore!

And eyes there were that filled with Love's
     own tears;
   And lips that proudly swore
To love past death a thousand, thousand years!
For in that land no treachery came, nor fears, —
   The Land of Nevermore!

'T is gone — 't is faded — vanished from us quite;
   Naught can its joys restore;
Black wings wave round us of the coming night;
We walk within the shadow of its might, —
   The Land of Nevermore!

Avenged

A FRIGHTENED moon, without one star,
   Close chased by demon clouds;
Gaunt castle ruins, dim and far,
   Where phantoms flit in shrouds;
Fierce winds that torture frantic trees,
   And fright the guilty grass;
The moanings of sepulchral seas;
   Weird spectres, that repass;
Black umbrage, threatening unknown doom;
   Old blood-stains on the moss;
Pallid above a grave's damp gloom,
   The white and ghostly cross.
No hint of hidden human guilt,
   Save this, the ghouls impart:
A dagger — to the jewelled hilt, —
   Rusts in a woman's heart.

ARROWS OF EROS

Trifles, light as air
— SHAKESPEARE

Oh, Not on the Field

THE SOLDIER'S SONG

OH, not on the field of conquest red,
  Where the crimsoned victors lay, —
Not there with my laurels round my head,
Not there in my glory find me dead,
  Not there — not there, I pray!

Not on the deck where we conquer and bleed,
  Conquer, and sink in the sea;
Find me not there — not there, I plead —
Wrapped in the shroud of the gray sea-weed,
  Ah, not in the arms of the sea!

Not in the sea, in its restless bed;
  And not in the war's alarms;
But here, Beloved, here, instead,
Let the whole world find me, when I am dead,
  In the white coil of thine arms!

The Captive

THE KNIGHT'S SONG

THE arrow on the tower vane
  Is pointing to the sea;
The castle's gargoyles gurgle rain
  All week, incessantly;
And in the dove-cote, doves remain
  In forced captivity.

O Love! let the sweet storm abide
  That keeps me here by thee,
The gargoyles gush with rain, and hide
  The whole world and the sea —
For in our dove-cote, by thy side,
  Dear is captivity!

Her Roses

THE LOVER'S SONG

I

ONE day when I was standing by
    My gentle little Maid,
I took the roses from her hand
    Within the wildwood shade;
I stooped above her, where she sat
    Upon the rock to rest,
And let the petals flutter down
    The dimples of her breast.

II

O rose-leaves — O my rose-leaves red,
    Quite vanished from mine eyes,
She 'll find you when her couch she seeks,
    There in your paradise;
While I, a-wandering through the night
    Alone in rain and wind,
Shall bless myself if I may see
    Her shadow on the blind!

Lovers in the Lane

THE POET'S SONG

As arm in arm they passed anear,
    The maiden and her lad,
Their beauty pierced me as a spear,
    Their joyance made me sad.

Then felt I like the evening cloud,
    That in the sunset skies
Sees round it float a beauteous crowd,
    While it dissolves and dies.

Ah, beauty gives us cruel stings
    When grown in others' bowers;
And youth and love are bitter things
    When they 're no longer ours !

Sirens

A-POISE upon the mullein's tipmost top,
  And bending down its rod of gold,
The thistle-finch all liquidly lets drop
  Melodies manifold.

At sunset, in the laurel underbrush,
  From roseate blooms beneath the trees,
Upon the silence pours th' impassioned thrush
  Rapturous ecstasies.

But when Lucella, sweeter than them all,
  Warbles within the starry night,
Her words are silver orbs of song, that fall
  Thrillingly exquisite !

The Moon-Ship

O MID-DAY Moon, that in the blue of June
    Movest so fair above ;
Art thou the phantom ship that all too soon
    Didst take away my love?

If thou art she, pale wanderer, then to me,
    When thou dost next arise,
Oh, bring her back again, that I may see
    The love-light of her eyes !

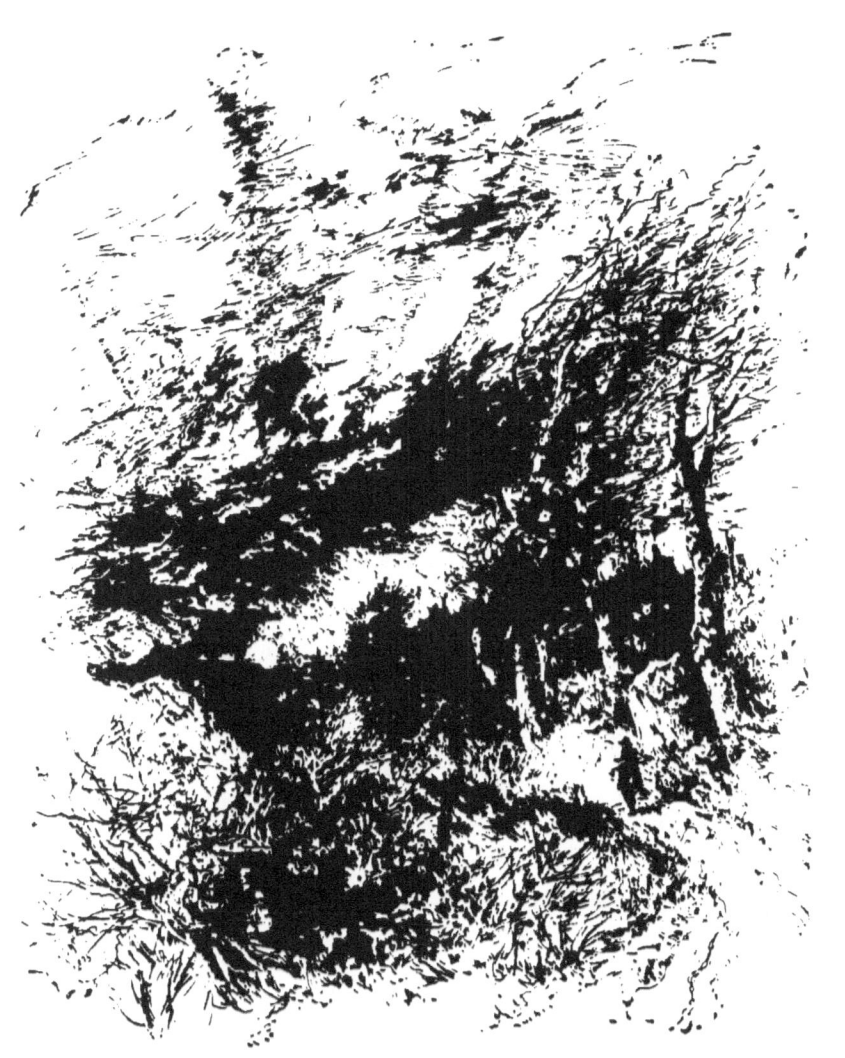

Sink down, O lurid sun!

Betrayed

SINK down the leaden sky, O sun,
  With all thy lurid light, —
  The dismal day is done;
Thy rising raised me from the deep,
  Thy setting brings me night,
And makes me, loveless, weep, —
  Sink down, O lurid sun!

.

In Pall-Mall

1872

Alieni temporis flores

REMEMBER you the day we were to meet,
    When I, in London, was a loiterer ;
    And you, all muffled in a wealth of fur,
    Came tripping with your Cinderella feet,
Through the cold drizzle that was almost sleet,
    Bringing a sense of warmth and lavender?
    And then, 'neath one umbrella, how we were
    Drenched, but most happy, wading down the
        street?
What did it matter all the mud and slush?
    What did it matter should love bring us pain?
    Your voice was like the gurgle of a thrush —
Your voice, that I shall never hear again !
    Your lips, your eyes, your dimples and your
        blush —
    Whose *are* they, since I 've left the London rain?

The Lunch al Fresco

Paris 1872

Agnosco veteris vestigia flammæ

WHAT was to me the most delicious wine? . . . ·
  Ah, yes! 't was that I sipped at Fontainebleau;
  You were sixteen, and I an ardent beau;
  Children in love, and each to each, divine;
I was your world, and you, I said, were mine :
  No lovers *ever* loved each other so —
  We stopped and swore it by the beech, you know.
  At last we ope'd our bottle, — we would dine —
But glasses had we none — what should we do?
  We took it, gurgling, in alternate sips,
  Straight from the flask, — a laughing, loving pair;
Then, while the wine was wet upon your lips,
  I kissed them, and . . . how long it seems ago! . . .
  The wine? Ah, Love! the *wine* was "*ordinaire!*"

In Pall-Mall

1872

Alieni temporis flores

REMEMBER you the day we were to meet,
   When I, in London, was a loiterer ;
   And you, all muffled in a wealth of fur,
   Came tripping with your Cinderella feet,
Through the cold drizzle that was almost sleet,
   Bringing a sense of warmth and lavender?
   And then, 'neath one umbrella, how we were
   Drenched, but most happy, wading down the
      street?
What did it matter all the mud and slush?
   What did it matter should love bring us pain?
   Your voice was like the gurgle of a thrush —
Your voice, that I shall never hear again!
   Your lips, your eyes, your dimples and your
      blush —
   Whose *are* they, since I 've left the London rain?

The Lunch al Fresco

Paris 1872

Agnosco veteris vestigia flammæ

WHAT was to me the most delicious wine? . . . ·
  Ah, yes! 't was that I sipped at Fontainebleau;
  You were sixteen, and I an ardent beau;
  Children in love, and each to each, divine;
I was your world, and you, I said, were mine:
  No lovers *ever* loved each other so —
  We stopped and swore it by the beech, you know.
  At last we ope'd our bottle, — we would dine —
But glasses had we none — what should we do?
  We took it, gurgling, in alternate sips,
  Straight from the flask, — a laughing, loving pair;
Then, while the wine was wet upon your lips,
  I kissed them, and . . . how long it seems ago! . . .
  The wine? Ah, Love! the *wine* was "*ordinaire!*"

97

My Source of Light

SONG

I 'M like the gray cloud just above
  The dawn ere day 's begun;
And thou 'rt my source of light, my Love,
  Thou art my morning sun.

Pale am I till I feel thy beam,
  Till life thy light bestows;
And then a golden cloud I seem,
  Bathed in ethereal rose!

Take Back Your Words

SONG

Take back your words and dry your tears,
  Life is too short for hate;
We may be dead a thousand years, —
  Yet Love can conquer Fate.
Too soon, alas! each golden head
  Shall lie beneath the clay; —
What feelings have the silent dead? . . .
  Oh, love the while you may!

For life is like a drop of rain,
  So small its limits be;
But death is monstrous as the main —
  The myriad-millioned sea.
Give me your lips; dry all your tears;
  So we at last may say,
If we are dead a thousand years
  At least we 've loved to-day!

By the Frozen River

A WINTER SONG

I

THE river's surface, icy-mailed,
  Has bound the boat and oar,
And Winter reigns where Summer failed : —
O Love, remember how we sailed
  Along this very shore !

II

The frost our currents, too, assailed ;
  No Spring can them restore ;
The tears, the vows, — ah, naught availed : —
O Love, remember how we sailed
  Where we shall sail no more !

And Winter reigns where Summer failed

Far from the Dawn

TO M. B. G.

AN EVENING SONG

THE evening light is waning low
  · Above the wooded hills ;
The only note within the air
  The lonely whippoorwill's.
The prima donna of the dawn,
  The golden-throated lark,
All songless in the dale, alone,
  Awaits the coming dark.

O Love, at morn, refulgent thou,
  At eve, how dim, in sooth !
Ah, where has all the music flown
  That filled the fields of youth ?
Now lower sinks the evening light,
  And lonelier loom the hills;
With not a note in all the air, —
  Not e'en the whippoorwill's !

From Dawn till Dusk

SONG

I

As down the clover path I wade
  All in the morning sun,
I pass the stile within the glade,
  And then I think of one, —
  Oh, then I think of one!

II

At noon, when Summer days are bright,
  As, musing by the run,
I see the water-lilies white,
  Oh, then I think of one, —
  Oh, then I think of one!

III

When through the twilight fields I go
  After the day is done,
I look into the West, and oh!
  'T is then I think of one, —
  'T is then I think of one!

Where Have They Gone

SONG

WHERE are the rims of the beautiful hills
   That gladdened our eyes as we walked?
And where are the woods and the woodland rills
   Where we sat by the hour and talked?

Oh, where are the birds that sang in the dell
   So tenderly, soft, and low,
That we paused in the love we had to tell
   And listened, — how long ago!

In Drear November

IF to me the night is so steeped in gloom,
  With sobbings of rain
  On the window-pane —
Who sit by the warmth of my fire-lit room —
  Oh ! what must it be
  To sweet Marjorie,
Adown in that desolate marsh-land tomb !

Go on with the Play

SONG

I

LET the play go on as is meet,
  We will smile and endure it yet;
But the roses of life are far less sweet
  Than the lilies of regret.

II

Oh, gone is the love and the trust;
  She sleeps by the willow-tree;
And only a handful of mouldering dust
  Is the heart that broke for me.

III

Go on with the play as is meet,
  We will smile and endure it yet;
But the roses of life are far less sweet
  Than the lilies of regret!

The Crescent

JUST over the gates of the gold and glow
    Where the sunset spirits are,
She floats in the nebulous amber, low,
Luminous, languorous, moving slow,
    Away from the evening star.

A golden cloud drifts back from her face
    Like the tress of her yellow hair;
And the stars come out of their hiding-place
To bask in her beauty and feel her grace, —
    To woo her, she is so fair.

Her answers are soft as adagios,
    Yet wayward and coy is she;
When the petals close of the western rose,
Evading them all, she silently goes
    Over the edge of the sea!

MINOR CHORDS

I touch the silent strings,
*   The broken lute complains ;*
The sweets of love are gone,
*   The bitterness remains.*
        —RICHARD HENRY STODDARD

Blight

HAPPY are they, who, loving lovely things,
    Each new day love them more;   .
Whose tranquil spirits bear no restive wings, —
    Who dwell, but never soar.

There falls on certain souls this heavy doom,
    And wraps the morn in night:
Joy's grape, once touched, will bear no second bloom,
    Nor old stars yield their light.

Above the Trees

I

THE fields are fair with waving wheat;
The earth is blooming round my feet;
But, oh, that blue I love to greet,
    Above the trees!

II

How much of all that seemed most bright,
How much I've loved and lost, has quite
Evanished, — passed far out of sight, —
    Above the trees!

III

No wonder, if, at morning red,
At noon, or when the day is dead,
I pause, oft-times, and gaze o'erhead,
    Above the trees!

Hollyhocks

Thoughts that do often lie too deep for tears — WORDSWORTH

I

THEY rise beyond the fountain rocks,
These spinsters robed in dainty frocks,
    So stately, prim, and tall;
Their hue the very rainbow mocks, —
These quaint, old-fashioned hollyhocks
    Against my garden wall.

II

Their crimson e'en the rose defies;
Their pink is like the morning skies
    While yet the sun is low;
And if we turn away our eyes
They hold us with their witcheries
    And will not let us go.

III

Too coarse to cull for a bouquet,
And lacking fragrance, yet do they
 Compel us still to see;
And as the breezes make them sway,
What ribboned maidens are so gay
 In dance upon the lea!

IV

And when I look the garden through,
And mark, against the mountain's blue,
 The noon upon them bright,
I know not how it be with you,
But as for me it is a true
 And exquisite delight!

V

The poet whose imaginings
Soar upward on ethereal wings
 The higher realms to reach,
Is melted by the simplest things;
And e'en a garden flower brings
 Dreams beyond song or speech.

VI

The hands that set these posies here
Are turned to dust this many a year, —
   So soon our dearest die!
O Memory, in this nether sphere,
What art thou but a constant tear
   That rises to Love's eye!

The Knight, the Maid, and the Minstrel

I

Soft, my steed, across the sward; neigh not when
the bugle calls.
Cease a-clanging, shield and sword, we are near her
castle walls.
Hold thy breath, O twilight breeze, let the long grass
sink to rest
There beneath ancestral trees: Lo! she standeth in
the West, —

II

Standeth on her turret high, dark against the setting
sun;
Pensive, as the knights go by gay with plume and
gonfalon.
Circled with her yellow hair, like the glory round a
star,
Often in the evening air have I seen her from afar, —

III

From afar, but never near, mute as marble — so she
　seems —
Musing on some cavalier, down the green lanes of
　her dreams.
Ah! if she but dreamed of me, what a joy were then
　the strife!
I could ride down Destiny in the clashing lists of
　life!

IV

Kings, for her, would give a realm; I, a knight, would
　brave disgrace;
Court a lance-thrust through the helm, for the sake
　of such a face.
" Maiden with the lustrous hair, dimly seen at dusk
　of day,
Underneath those lashes fair, are there eyes of blue
　or gray?

V

" Blue or gray or shadowy brown? Lift them, prithee,
    let them speak;
And the roses newly blown in the garden of thy
    cheek,
Are they blushes meant for me? If for other knight
    they bloom,
By thy beauty's witchery, tell me, Damsel, tell for
    whom! . . .

VI

"Silent as a moorland flower! Cruel Maid, I might
    as soon
On a dial learn the hour by the light of Merlin's
    moon.
Baffled thus each eventide, shall I, wondering what
    thou art,
Ever solve, as on I ride, that sweet riddle called thy
    heart?"

VII

" Nay, Sir Knight, be not so bold ! " Here her Harper, like a cloud,
Rose beside her, gray and old, swept his harp, and spake aloud :
" Nay, Sir Knight, be thou reproved. Let the mystery alone.
Lo, the maiden shall be loved better that she be not known.

VIII

" Looming o'er Life's desert sands, Cupid's gilded domes arise ;
See, when touched with human hands, how they crumble from the skies !
Will the heart of youth n'er learn, Love that beckons with his torch,
Beckons but to scathe and burn, — burn, and blind, and sear, and scorch ?

IX

" Thou shalt keep aloof for aye ; she, above all search
　　or quest, —
Half the perfume flies away, when the rose is once
　　possessed.
Thou, O maiden, like a star, still a mystic vision
　　seem ;
On thy turret keep afar ; be to him a beauteous dream.

.

X

" Hear thy Minstrel's prophecy, — red the words rise
　　from his heart, —
Lovers who would love for aye, must forever love
　　apart."

.　　.　　.　　.　　.　　.　　.　　.　　.

So they parted, as was doomed ; but, if legends run
　　aright,
In each heart a lily bloomed — bloomed eternal, day
　　and night.

The Singer

SORROW had marred her face, — how much !
   And dimmed her wondrous eyes ;
But, oh, her Voice ! — her voice it could not touch,—
   That was of Paradise.

Longfellow

Nihil tetigit quod non ornavit

NOT in the dawning of his golden prime
　His finest songs across the world he flung;
But who could match the pathos of his rhyme,
　When that the eve of life around him hung?

As darkness neared, rarer each touching lay;
　Then, through his lyre, we heard his rapt soul pour:
As those charmed harps that but at night-time play
　Æolian strains on Pascagoula's shore.

The Watcher

Not a break in the gray East's dungeon bars,
   Where the dawn lies prisoned behind the clouds;
And the dome is dark with the graves of stars,
   As muffled they lie in their sable shrouds.

Alone I wait on the black cliff's brow,
   With my pale hands stretched to the unseen sea;
While the breakers moan in the mist below,
   And beat, like the heart that beats in me.

But when to the soul did the sea sing hope?
   The sea-god is dumb.   So I stand and wait
For the prophet lips of the Dawn to ope,
   And banish, or brighten, the face of Fate.

Far better to drowse on the dim sweet breast
   Of the starless Night, with her slumberous eyes,
Than to watch forever, in aching quest,
   For a glimmer of day in the dawnless skies.

O passionate arms, are ye faint on the height?
   O fervent lips, will ye cease to pray?
Lo, the morn is past, yet it brought no Light;
   And the noon comes on, but it brings no Day.

To a Baby

B. M. B.

BABY, Fay, or wingless Sprite,
Wanderer from supernal light,
  Fragment of the Infinite,
Shake the star-dust from your curls,
Tell us — older boys and girls —
  Of the land that love empearls.

We forget — for we grow old
All the shining ways of gold,
  All the anthems upward rolled;
We forget the silver note
Of the cherubs as they float,
  Nimbus'd in the air remote.

Tell us of that City bright,
With its precious stones bedight,—
  Jasper, jacinth, chrysolite.
We forget how looked the skies;
Tell us of the land that lies
  O'er the walls of Paradise!

A Winter Dirge

M. B. M.

How white and still o'er tomb and post
  The moon-made shadows go, —
The trailing garments of a ghost,
  Across the church-yard snow.

And does she feel the season's change, —
  The maid who sleeps below?
And seems it sweet, or seems it strange,
  The roses — then the snow?

Ah, let it hail and let it roar,
  Or let the roses blow;
Alas! she recks not any more,
  Asleep beneath the snow!

Roland to the Nun

I

THE pain I suffer for her is more sweet
   Than all the joys that love e'er gave before;
Better to touch the blue veins of her feet,
   Than loveliest lips that beauty ever bore.

II

Let others fold a fair form full of bliss;
   Let others thrill the senses, one and all;
But, oh, my white Dove, I would kneel and kiss
   Even your shadow on the convent wall!

Is there no balm of sweet repose

Beyond the Hills

THE morning comes; the evening goes;
Sick of life's petty joys and woes,
I crave the rest that peace bestows.
Is there no balm of sweet repose
     Beyond the hills?

O watcher on the peaks of white,
Seest thou no rays of coming light, —
No rifts of day within the night?
Will the Dawn bring me my delight,
     Beyond the hills?

Beneath the Palm

NEAR Appalachicola's reef,
Upon the floating lily leaf,
  The adder sleeps at noon;
And from the tangles of the brake,
The larum of the rattlesnake
  Startles the still lagoon.

On Okeechobee's waters black,
At eve the alligator's back
  Floats huge and dark and bare;
Meanwhile, the sweet magnolia bloom
Drifts o'er the venom and the doom
  That lie in ambush there.

Ah, region of the tropic bowers,
The quest of youth, — the land of flowers,
  By Pensacola's bay;
A land such as no other seems,
Thou livest only in our dreams, —
  De Leon's Florida!

The Road

Oh, the sweet o' the day is its mystery,
  And I trudge the old road still;
I shall never be happy until I can see
  Over the brow of the hill.

Oh, Life with its mysteries dark and high,
  Who shall explore its steeps?
I crave to fathom the fathomless sky,
  And of Death, the bottomless deeps.

Ah, the sweet o' the day is its mystery,
  But I trudge the old road still;
And shall never be happy until I can see
  Over the brow of the hill!

They Bring Their Flowers

I

THEY bring their flowers,
They weep a little o'er us
  In our narrow bed;
How soon their lips shall find
Some kiss more dear than ours,
  When we are dead!

II

'T is no surprise
That sweeter smiles will come,
  When our worn smile is sped;
That those who loved us once
Shall love more lustrous eyes,
  When we are dead.

III

Be not deceived
E'en by love's protestations
   Round the dying bed;
That some would miss us living
Well may be believed, —
   How few, when dead!

IV

If strong and fair,
We may be loved, perhaps,
   While beauty's rose is red;
But oh, how soon forgot,—
How little do they care,
   When we are dead!

My Father at Eighty

I SAW him sitting in his sunset chair;
His eyes were gazing fondly into space;
I did not speak; I knew that, hovering there,
He saw again my mother's long-lost face.

A Poet's Bookcase

OH, gently, — gently near the bookcase tread;
  Speak only in hushed whispers, soft and low;
These are the urns that hold the deathless dead,
  The souls of those passed onward long ago.

At this still shrine your heart-felt homage give;
  With reverence touch each tome upon the shelves;
These are the Dreams of Genius, — hence they live, —
  The fine quintessence of their finer selves.

The Anniversary

THE silent snow is on the land,
　The moon is shining bright;
I take the roses in my hand,
　And tread the path of white.

Ah, life belongs alone to youth,
　And we of riper years,
But walk a wistful way of ruth
　Along a stream of tears.

What use for roses have I now,
　Who miss what love once gave?
Only to stoop, and in the snow,
　To lay them on her grave!

My Lady Fair

OX-EYED daisy, in the grass,
   Looking in that queenly way,
Come, I cannot by you pass,
   I must cull you here to-day.
'T is because your glowing crown
   Calls to mind, as I behold,
Her great eyes of velvet brown,
   And her hair of wondrous gold.

Laurel blooms that here recline,
   Growing on the wooded crest,
Verily you must be mine,
   I will wear you on my breast.
Know you why each coral star
   From your branches here I clip?
'T is because to me you are
   Rosy as my Lady's lip.

Elder blossoms white as snow,
   Flowering by the meadow fence,
Longer here you may not grow,
   Surely I must take you hence.
Why should I with half a sigh
   Break you off in spite of ruth?
'T is because you seem to me
   Pure as is my Lady's truth.

Everything of loveliness, —
   Bird and blossom, perfumed air, —
Makes me think of her, and bless
   One so gentle and so fair.
Who is she such solace gives?
   Who so beauteous and so kind?
Ah! my Lady only lives
   In the palace of my mind.

O What Is Song

O WHAT is Song,
And what is Art,
And what is Fame
    To me, —
Who sit apart,
With single heart,
    In loveless ecstasy?

Ah, what are Hearts
When once possessed;
Ah, what are Loves
    To me, —
In whose dark breast
A sea's unrest
    Pulses eternally?

O what is Life,
And what are Dreams,
And what is Death
    To me, —
What, but dull beams, —
But hints and gleams
    Of grander Entity!

The Bride of the Sea

IN MEMORY OF JAMES JACKSON JARVES — FLORENCE

THERE are cities high over Orion
  That jasper and sardonyx be;
Whose streets it were joy but to lie on,
  Whose walls it were bliss but to see;
Many sumptuous cities fair Dian
  Beholds over mountain and lea,
But the Bride, 'neath the wings of her Lion, —
  Where is one such as she?

She is crowned with her triumphs and towers,
  And blue run the veins in her arms;
Like the lotus, afloat with her flowers,
  Her whiteness hath wonderous charms;
Delicious her lips are, with powers
  Circean, yet void of alarms;
And the mortal that dreams of her bowers
  Leaves his soul in her arms.

Yet should time, ever eager, though olden,
  Her fairness despoil and depose ;
Should her domes, which at evening are
    golden,
  Dissolve as her Apennine snows ;
Should the sceptre, which long she hath
    holden,
  Depart, and the crown from her brows,
And the robes of her splendor be rolled in
  The gray dust of her woes ;

Should the glory grow dim of her Titians,
  Her gondolas drift 'neath the moon ;
Should her marbles, mosaics, Venetians,
  Evanish and pass as a swoon ;
Should her forehead, the fairest of visions,
  Sink under the silent lagoon,
And the sea, tombing all her traditions,
  Leave a waste for the loon ;

Should she melt as a mist evanescent,
    Or fade as a myth from a scroll, —
Yet her wraith would arise juvenescent,
    Aglow with a great aureole ;
Still her glamour, eternally crescent,
    Supreme o'er the spirit would roll;
And her Name, as a star iridescent,
    Light the sky of the soul.

Though in regions celestial there are lands —
    Bright lands it were bliss but to see,
Whose towers, built high over star lands,
    Of beryl and sardonyx be ;
Though cities in fabulous far lands
    Loom fair over mountain and lea, —
Yet on earth, in her gloom, or her garlands,
    Who so comely as she !

The Wing of Death

WE stood beside the church-yard stone,
　My pale sweetheart and I;
We mused a moment there alone;
　A tear was in her eye.
I took her by the trembling hand,
　And kissed away the tear;
I wondered which of us would stand
　Above the other's bier.

She read my thought, and quick she said,
　" I 'm but a woman — I,
But on the day I saw you dead,
　That day I, too, should die."
I laughed it off, to hide the blow —
　It is a way with men —
Alas! how little did we know
　That *she* was dying then!

Ode to the Memory of Keats

1880

I

THY voice is as the sound of far-off seas,
And sweeter than the hum of Enna's bees,
That fed on flowers round the milk-white knees
Of hapless Proserpina; or than strains
Of harps æolian, made by murmurous leaves
When elfin airs are going through green lanes
    In some enchanted vale;
Or than a song at sunset, 'mid the sheaves,
When troops of reapers, singing, ope the bars,
And the young crescent with her sister stars,
    Stoops low to listen, golden pale; —
    Sweeter than all these!
And softer than the sound of waters falling
Through dells of El Dorado; or the calling
Of rose-limbed Nymphs, at eve, for their god lover
Among the trees Idalian, arching over
Dim avenues whose twilights never change;
Ah! sweeter than all things we may discover,
    And strange! —

Strange as the song of some unrestful star
That falls above a city, but so far
And high, none hear, save those who watch the
    skies
A-hunger for the eternal harmonies
That drop from lips of haloed poets dead, —
    So sounds thy voice o'erhead ;
And, listening, lesser Bards hear the rapt tone,
Harp sweeter songs, and think the strains their
    own,
    So Orphean-sweet thine are !

II

    Unread may rest thy lays
      For many days —
    For many weary years ;
And yet their echo still is in our ears,
    And sounds within our soul,
Like the dim-heard, far-off, faint thunder-roll
    Along the evening hills.

III

Thou wast the Muse's favored one,
Whose syllables were as a benison
    To heal our mortal ills.

Thou who didst honey from Hymettus rob,
Thou, in the mind's celestial Parthenon,
Hast filled thy niche, where all about thy lips
  The stone glows with white eloquence,
   Making the silence throb.
Yet, O sweet poet, — thou who liest hence
Under that slab pathetically small,
Like one white lily thrown outside the wall,
Upon the Roman grass, — this was thy doom:
Within a callous people's laggard tomb,
  Which is henceforth, to us, a shrine,
   To lie forgotten long;
   Silent those lips of thine,
  Nurtured upon Olympian wine,
Wet at the Heliconian spring divine,
And made immortal by immortal song.

     IV

Aërial architect, whose realm was space,
Who in the mind's blue zenith — thine abode —
Reared the transcendent spire of the Ode;
Who built dream-raftered temples, high and strong,
That break life's flat horizon into joy, —
The Brunelleschi of the Dome of Song, —
A full-voiced poet thou, while yet a boy.

Thy lips true sculptors were, and, gay or grave,
The plastic language took the print they gave;
Apollo touched them, and beyond recall,
Thy speech thereafter ran most musical
Through all its lucent labyrinthine ways, —
 Through all thy golden lays.
But Atropos, too soon, with sudden shears
Above thee leaned to cut thy thread of years,
 And as she cut it, sighed;
  Thereat thy name
   Died
  Into deathless fame!

    v

  O weak, — yet strong!
  Pale Star of later Song,
  Across the Atlantic, streams
 The glorious splendor of thy beams,
Reaching and dazzling many an eye and ear.
And still thou liv'st. We feel thy joys and ills;
Thy spirit walketh on our sunset hills;
Thy lays yet breathe, to those who still can hear,
Memnonian music from auroral air;
Thy voice is on the peaks, serene and clear;
From Indian dells, or down Ionian dales,

We hear thy harp still sighing Grecian tales
  Of deities melodiously forlorn, —
We hear, — and bless the day that thou wast born.
O Poet of the night, and of the morn,
      Bard of immortal woes,
Thou mad'st our world more beauteous and more
    sweet,
And so we cast our pearls about thy feet
      In reverence, with a sigh;
We who love beauty cannot let thee die;
We know thy heart was pierced through with the
    thorn,
      Though hidden by the rose;
·We know thy breast was bleeding all life long,
O thou, the Nightingale of English Song!

The Idealists

TO THE MEMORY OF THOS. BUCHANAN READ

I

As a cloud that dissolves in the sky
　At the close of the day,
Even so out of life, silently,
　Man passes away.
As a leaf from the branch of a tree
　Falls and melts in the mould,
So for man — the godlike and free —
　This fate is foretold.

ii

As the tussocks on prairie or plain
　Are swallowed by fire,
So of man, but his ashes remain, —
　The earth is his pyre.
All his work, all his love, all his fame, —
　Verse, picture, or bust, —
'T is a dream, 't is a wraith, 't is a name,
　It is dust, it is dust!

III

Yet no less will we strive to the end,
　E'en if life has deceived;
Let death prove a foe or a friend,
　We strove, we achieved.
With humility haughty as pride,
　Looking up through our bars,
As we lived and aspired, so we died, —
　Athirst for the stars!

Mariners

A HYMN

DARKNESS upon the vast;
  Storm raging wild around;
Torn sail, and shattered mast, —
  Far thunder-sound!

No harbor-lamps to-night;
  Waves dashing o'er the deck;
Fierce breakers surging white,
  Warning of wreck!

Louder the billows roar;
  Wilder the waters leap;
Lost — lost in sight of shore —
  Lost in the deep!

Lo, on the furious sands,
  Death waits upon the coast;
Help, Lord! reach out Thy hands
  Ere we are lost!

God of the storm and sea,
  Sink we, unless Thou save, —
Fill us with faith in Thee
  To walk the wave!

    .   .   .   .   .   .

See where, to aid us, He
  Comes through the raging blast. . . .
O Star of Galilee! —
  Saved! . . . Saved at last!

Across the Years

TO E. H.

YE Poets of all the ages and climes,
   I know the bent of your song;
In Summer, right gay were your golden rhymes,
   And dark, when the Winter was long.

When Spring was queen of the redolent year,
   In verdure your verses were clad;
When Fall, like a lorn dove, fluttered drear,
   The notes that you crooned were sad.

O Poets of every æon and clime,
   Your singing is naught but a breath; . . .
I hear the desolate surges of Time
   Sob on the shores of Death!

Footfalls on the Stairs

I

WHEN morning from the clouds of roseate red
Comes with her dewy and delicious airs,
I rise and leave my solitary bed,
And stepping softly, hear the muffled tread
    Of footfalls on the stairs.

II

When through the lonely house at noon I go,
Wrapped in deep thought, and troubled with my
        cares,
Pacing the floors in silence to and fro,
I hear those feathery sounds, so soft and low —
    The footfalls on the stairs.

III

At twilight, when the lamps make solemn cheer,
When each loved portrait recognition wears —
Pictures of lost ones beyond measure dear —
As through the halls I pass, I pause, and hear
    Faint footfalls on the stairs.

IV

Àt midnight, when I mount up to my room,
And shadows from my glimmering light that flares
Walk with me, and above me darkly loom,
I listen, for I hear from out the gloom
    The footfalls on the stairs.

V

After the heart is stript and desolate;
After the losses, sorrows, sobs, and prayers;
After the loneliness of life's long wait, —
Oh, may I hear within the Golden Gate
    Those footfalls on the stairs!

NOTES

PAGE 27. — Calliope is here used as a general name for the Muse of Poetry.

PAGE 59. — The picture upon which this sonnet is written is a copy of a Cuyp in the author's possession, not an original, as might be inferred from the caption of the sonnet.

PAGE 67. — An English writer of distinction, — himself a poet, — having seen this sonnet in MS., writes to the author: "In England we pronounce Euganean with the *e* long; but it is of course wrong to do so. It is Shelley's fault; he rhymed it to *pæan*, forgetting Martial's line: '*Nupsit ad Euganeos sola puella lacus.*'"

PAGE 78. — Line eleven. The author has here made use of a superstition current among the negroes of the Southern States.

PAGE 93. — Here, and on page 71, an experiment in rhythm has been attempted; and this is really the *raison d' être* of the two little poems.

PAGE 138. — By permission of Lippincott's Magazine.